Daft Dog

With much love to CC

First published in Great Britain by HarperCollins Publishers Ltd in 1999

1 3 5 7 9 10 8 6 4 2

ISBN: 0-00-198209-5

Printed and bound in Singapore by Imago

Daft Dog

Colin and Jacqui Hawkins

Collins

An Imprint of HarperCollinsPublishers

This is Daft Dog.

Daft Dog was always getting things WRONG. Sometimes he would brush his fur with the bath brush,

wash his face with toothpaste, and clean his teeth with soap.

Each morning, when Daft Dog got dressed
he never seemed to get things right. He put
his jumper on back to front,
his shoes on the wrong
feet and his socks
never matched.
"I never know
if I'm coming
or going," said
Daft Dog.

One morning, Daft Dog went shopping.
In the fish shop he asked for a new pair of
slippers. "You are daft, Daft Dog, you're in the
wrong shop," laughed Mr Flipper the fishmonger.
"I don't sell slippers, but I do have a nice pair
of kippers."
"O.K.," said a puzzled Daft Dog, "I like kippers!"

Next Daft Dog went into the baker's, where he asked for a chocolate milk shake. "Ho! Ho!" laughed Mr Bun the baker. "You are funny, Daft Dog. You're in the wrong shop. I can't make you a milk shake, but I can sell you a delicious cream cake." "Yummy," said Daft Dog. "I do love cake."

Then Daft Dog asked the newsagent,
"Have you mended my shoes yet?"
"You are a daft dog.
I don't mend
shoes, but I do
sell the news,"
said Mr Rabbit.
"All right," said
Daft Dog and
he bought
a newspaper.

Later Daft Dog went to the shoe mender's and asked for some jellied eels. "What a daft dog," said Mr Boot the shoe mender, "I can't give you jellied eels, but you can have your shoes, soled and heeled. Daft Dog felt very confused.

That evening, Daft Dog got on the wrong
bus. He was soon completely lost and it
took him ages and ages to get back home.
"I don't know where I went wrong," said
Daft Dog.

The next day, Daft Dog went into the optician's.
He thought it was the library.
"Can you change
my book?"
he asked.

"Silly Daft Dog," laughed Mr Peepers the
optician, "I can't change your book, but I can
help you to look." And he fitted Daft Dog
with a pair of glasses. "WOW!" said Daft Dog.

In Mr Peeper's shop, Daft Dog loved all the different types of glasses...

reading glasses,

glasses on a stick,

glasses on a string,

sun glasses,

fun glasses.

"I can see I'm in the right shop now," laughed Daft Dog.

Now that he could see, Daft Dog wasn't half as daft as he had been.

In fact, Daft Dog was very clever...

he read lots and lots of books, spoke many languages and learnt how to play chess.

Daft Dog was now so clever that he went on T.V. and won *The Clever Clogs Dog Brain of the Year Quiz Show.* "I owe my spectacular success to my spectacles," said Daft Dog.

Nothing ever went WRONG any more for Daft Dog...

except, of course,
when he forgot his glasses!